C is for Colorado

written by kids for kids

WESTWINDS PRESS®

A is for Aspen

Aspen

Aspen trees turn gold and yellow. The breeze through their leaves is warm and mellow.

B is for **Boulder**

Boulder is a mountain town,
Perfect for riding your bike around.

C is for Camping

Sleeping under the gorgeous stars,
Getting away from the loud, noisy cars.

D is for **Denver**

Our Mile High City has a beautiful view,
And there is so much to see and do.

E is for Estes Park

I saw the haunted hotel and
skipped stones in the lake.
The leaves were all changing;
there were even snowflakes.

F

is for

Fourteeners

If you climb one of these
mountains so high,
It might feel like
you can touch the sky.

G is for Garden of the Gods

Kissing Camels, Siamese Twins,
Balanced Rock all alone:
These forms and more are found
in this garden of stone.

H is for Colorado Hairstreak

This butterfly is the insect of our state.
When they hatch each spring, I can hardly wait.

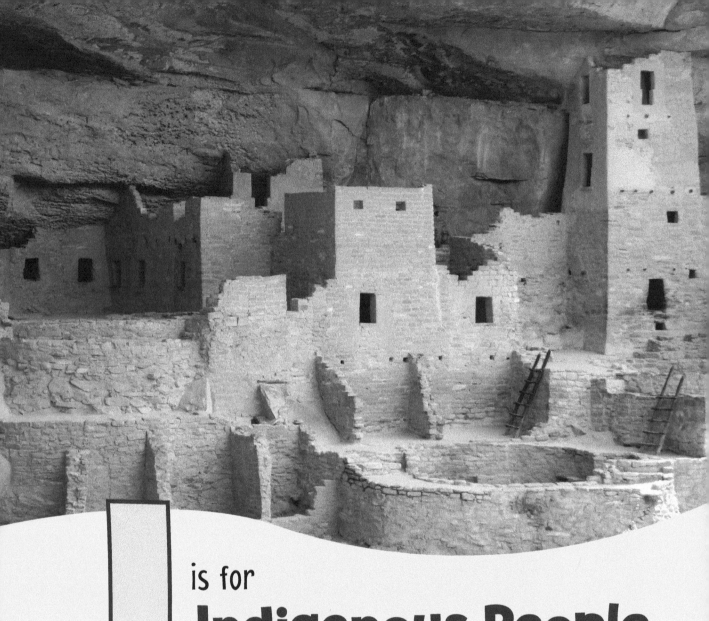

is for
Indigenous People

Many native peoples call this home—
The land where buffalo used to roam.

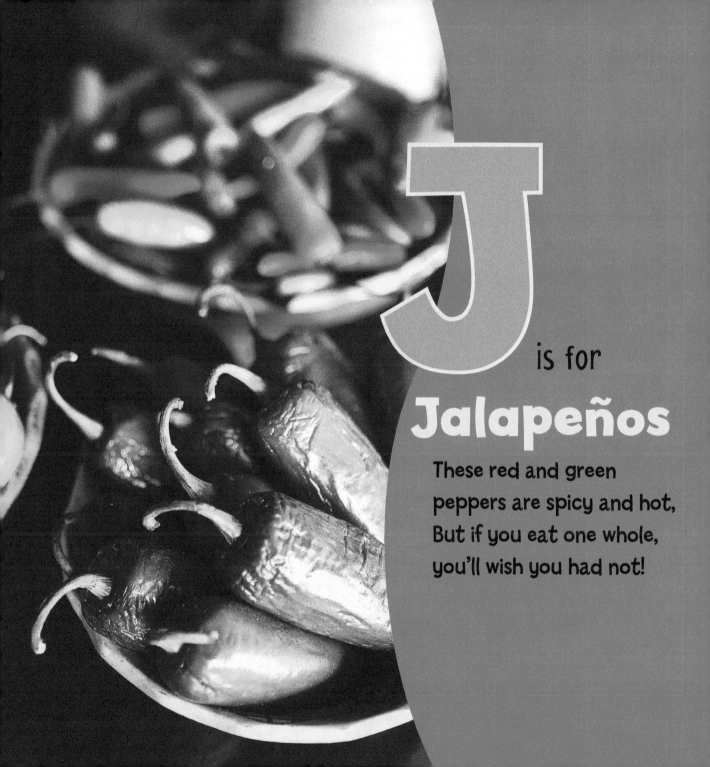

J
is for

Jalapeños

These red and green
peppers are spicy and hot,
But if you eat one whole,
you'll wish you had not!

K is for **Kayaking**

When you feel excitement lacking,
It must be time to go kayaking.

L

is for

Lark Bunting

Our state bird is known for its song.
I can listen to it sing all day long.

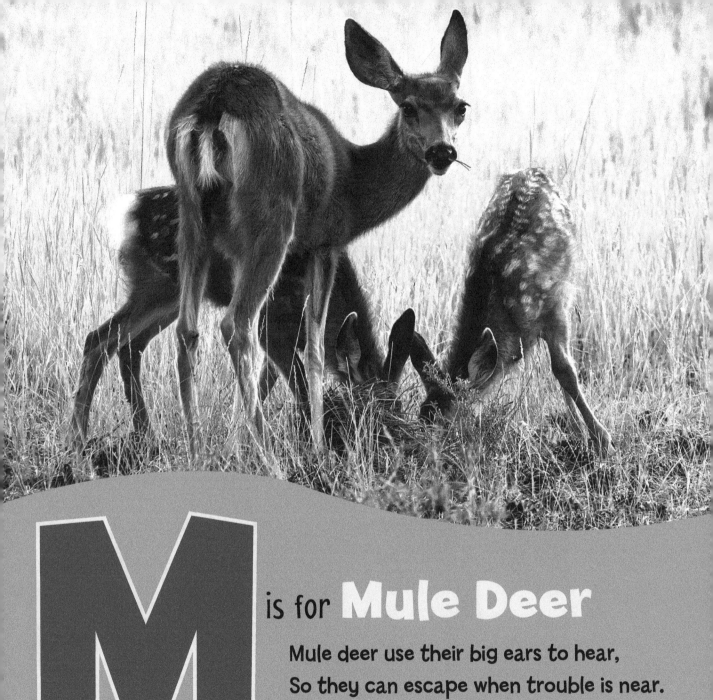

M is for Mule Deer

Mule deer use their big ears to hear,
So they can escape when trouble is near.

N

is for **Silver Nuggets**

Silver nuggets can be found
Deep in the mountains, underground.

O is for the Old West

The Old West is where the cowboys roamed—
Some moved around, some stayed in their homes.

P is for **Prairie Dog**

Prairie dogs on guard until day's end,
They let out a chirp to warn their friends.

is for **Quilt**

Patch by patch you tell
of days gone by,
And you keep me warm
in the middle of the night.

R

is for **Railroad**

The "iron horse" used
to be powered by steam,
Bringing folks here from
the east to find their dream.

S is for

Snowboarding

In the mountains you can
zoom down a hill.
It's winter and freezing,
but still it's a thrill.

T is for Telluride

When you're in Telluride you will be seeing
A whole lot of people skiing.

U is for Unpredictable Weather

Crazy weather, from storms to mild.
If you don't like it . . . just wait for a while.

V is for **Vail**

If you go and check out Vail,
Be sure to explore all their ski trails.

W

is for **Wildflower**

They make food from their leaves
and get water through their stems.
The Columbine is our state gem!

X is for eXtreme Sports

Kayak, heli-ski, rappel—
it's what Colorado's all about!
When you visit, you can try them out.

 is for

Yule Marble

Yule marble is found far and wide. Look closely, there's a sculpture waiting inside.

Z is for **Zebulon Pike**

We also know it as Pikes Peak,
If you climb it, you may feel weak.

Who Knew?

Aspen

Aspens grow in colonies: the trees start from a single seedling and spread by root suckers, like a strawberry plant. While one aspen tree can live up to 200 years, the root system of a colony can live for thousands of years!

Boulder

Boulder is for bookworms! The city has more used bookstores per person than any other city in the U.S. The first white people to settle the area weren't looking for books, however. They were looking for gold. The city started as a supply station for miners heading into the nearby mountains.

Camping

With four national parks and more than 40 state parks, Colorado is hard to beat for great camping spots! Did you know camping is the #1 outdoor activity in the U.S.? Yep. One in three Americans have given it a try. How about you? Most people who go camping, go with their kids!

Denver

Denver is one of the few cities in history that wasn't built near a road, railroad, or body of water. So what was it built near? The first flakes of gold that were found in 1858. And the city's first permanent building? A saloon!

Estes Park

Estes Park's spooky Stanley Hotel has ghosts for guests! Visitors can't sleep because of noisy ghost children playing in the halls, and Freelan Stanley, the man who built the hotel, keeps people entertained by playing piano in the music room . . . even though he's been dead for 70 years!

Fourteeners

Fourteeners are mountains more than 14,000 feet tall—that's ten times the height of the Empire State Building! Colorado has 54 fourteeners, the most in North America. Peak baggers, folks who try to climb all the fourteeners in a given area, are all over Colorado.

Garden of the Gods

Garden of the Gods got its name thanks to an argument. In the 1850s two surveyors checked out the incredible rock formations. One said, "Great place for a beer garden!" The other argued, "Beer garden? Why it is a place fit for the gods to assemble. We will call it 'Garden of the Gods!'" The name stuck.

Colorado Hairstreak

The Colorado hairstreak was chosen as the state insect by the 4th graders of Wheeling Elementary in Aurora. These beautiful purple butterflies lay their eggs on oak leaves and feed on tree sap and aphid honeydew. Yum-yum!

Indigenous People

Before white people arrived, many Indian tribes lived in the area that is now Colorado, including the Apache, Cheyenne, Comanche, Shoshone, and Ute. Some groups migrated through to hunt, while others made permanent settlements some of which you can still visit today.

Facts about the

Jalapeños

Just what makes jalapeños so hot? Capsaicin, a chemical found in the skin, seeds, and flesh of the pepper. Green jalapeños are the least spicy, red ones spicier, and dried jalapeños will burn your mouth off! But if you've got a cold, grab all the jalapeños you can find: these spicy wonders contain more vitamin C by weight than oranges!

Kayaking

Four thousand years ago indigenous peoples of the Arctic invented the first kayaks, which they used to hunt in lakes, rivers, and the ocean. The first kayaks were made from animal skins stretched over a driftwood frame. Wonder how those smelled?

Lark Bunting

The male lark bunting is quite the snazzy dresser. During mating season he has an elegant coat of black and white feathers, but in winter he turns a dull brown color. To protect his nesting territory, males fly way up in the air, then sing a mixture of whistles and trills as they dive-bomb down again. Watch out for kamikaze buntings!

Mule Deer

My, what big ears you have! A mule deer's giant ears give it extremely sensitive hearing. And if it hears you . . . BOING! It won't just run away, it will take bounding leaps, called "stotting," to escape you. Mule deer are quite the stotterers.

Silver Nuggets

Colorado used to be called "the Silver State" due to all the silver mining. You know silver is used in jewelry and coins, but did you know they use it in electronics, mirrors, and even medicine? Legends even tell of using silver to defeat vampires and werewolves! The world's largest silver nugget (approximately 2,000 pounds) was found in Aspen's Smuggler Mine in 1894.

The Old West

Just how old is the "Old West"? In the 1800s America's western border was the Mississippi River. Anything west of there was unknown territory, wild and lawless. We still refer to this area west of the Mississippi as the "Old West," even though it's practically in the middle of the country.

Prairie Dog

Prairie dogs got their name because of the doglike bark that they use to warn each other if danger is near. They are very social animals that live in large colonies, and when they greet each other they "kiss."

Quilt

Quilting has been around for hundreds of years. In the past, women took little scraps of leftover fabric from other sewing projects and put them together to create beautiful blankets. The largest historical quilt in the world is 11,390 square feet. That would cover 342 queen-sized beds!

great state of Colorado

Railroad

The growth of the railroads in the 1800s led to the growth of America. As rail lines expanded west, so did white settlers. In 1830 there were fewer than 80 miles of railroad track in the U.S. But by the end of the century, there were more than 160,000 miles of track. That would stretch more than halfway to the moon!

Snowboarding

Snowboarding has been around for about 30 years and it is now the fastest-growing sport in the world! Most snowboarders are 18 to 24 years old and 25 percent are women. Some fun snowboarding tricks: the Nosegrab (grab front lip of your board), Indy (grab toe side of board between feet), and McTwist (a 540-degree turn with a front flip).

Telluride

Gold was first discovered near Telluride in 1875 and as prospectors poured in, the town grew. The town was named after the chemical element tellurium, a gold-bearing ore that was never actually found there. Butch Cassidy's first major heist happened in Telluride when he robbed the San Miguel Valley Bank of about $20,000.

Unpredictable Weather

Although Colorado is blessed with an amazing 300 days of sunshine per year, it has its fair share of crazy weather: droughts, floods, lightning, hail, and even tornadoes. Colorado's got it all.

Vail

Vail is the #1 ski resort in the U.S. It has more miles of groomed trails than any other resort in the world. Pete Seibert, who founded the Vail Ski Resort in 1962, fell in love with the area when he trained there during WWII as part of the U.S. Army's 10th Mountain Division.

Wildflower

Colorado's state flower, the Rocky Mountain columbine, got its name from the Latin "columbinus," which means dove, because from the side or rear of the flower it resembles a group of doves. Beginning in 1925 the state government made it the duty of all Coloradoans to protect this fragile wildflower.

eXtreme Sports

Rafting, zip-lining, helicopter skiing, rock climbing, skydiving . . . Colorado's got more extreme sports than your average state. You might even say the adrenaline rush is a Colorado State of mind!

Yule Marble

Rock on! Yule marble is the state rock of Colorado and is found in the West Elk Mountains. It is famous for its pure white color. Other marbles are, well, more marbled (streaked with gray). The Yule marble deposit is one of the biggest and purest marbles ever found. Henry Bacon liked it so much he used it to build his most famous work: the Lincoln Memorial in Washington, D.C.

Zebulon Pike

Pikes Peak, the most visited mountain in North America, is named for Zebulon Pike, the explorer who "discovered" it in 1806. At 14,110 feet, it is one of the state's fourteeners. Believe it or not, thousands of runners speed up and down it every year—26 miles round-trip—during the Pikes Peak Marathon. Talk about your extreme sports!

T hank you to everyone at the Boys & Girls Clubs of Metro Denver for encouraging your kids to write and enter this contest. Thank you to the dedicated youth development staff, Emily Bobrick, Sarah Krieger, Stephanie Kugler, Helen McBain, George Patterson, Anthony Salazar, and Veronica Walker who guided the youth through this process and Tina Martinez for coordinating with the centers. And most of all, thanks to the kids who wrote such fantastic poetry for this book. Way to go!

Photo by Adrianna Santiago-Pass

Boys & Girls Clubs of Metro Denver is a youth development organization aimed at helping young people achieve academic success, develop good character and citizenship, and live healthy lifestyles. At the Clubs, youths benefit from a safe, positive environment, supportive relationships with caring adults and peers, a variety of fun programs and activities, opportunities and clear expectations, and recognition that reinforces success. To learn more about the Boys & Girls Clubs of Metro Denver, visit our Web site at www.positiveplacedenver.org.

Janely Altamirano, age 11 (A)

Destanie Fridley, age 12 (B)

Anastasia Lawrence, age 13 (C)

Damaryz Quijano, age 12 (D)

Jose Romo, age 13 (E)

Tahjeau Evans, age 13 (F)

Crystal Alfaro, age 11 (G)

Aniya Hickman, age 8 (H)

Felix Marrufo, age 11 (I)

Suzanna Guardado, age 13 &
   Abigail Guardado, age 12 (J)

Jesus Olivas, age 9 (K)

Viviana Carrillo, age 15 (L)

Mitzi Perez, age 10 (M)

Felix Marrufo, age 11 (N)

Marcus Serrano, age 12 (O)

Tony De La Loera, age 10 (P)

Makenri Richards, age 10 (Q)

Felicia Betcher, age 14 (R)

Maria Ricalday, age 10 (S)

Savanna Garza, age 9 (T)

Damaryz Quijano, age 12 (U)

Mary Martinez, age 11 &
   Savanna Garza, age 9 (V)

Chaliyah Love, age 6 (W)

Abigail Guardado, age 12 &
   Lazaro Chavez, age 12 (X)

Felix Marrufo, age 11 (Y)

Marcus Serrano, age 12 (Z)

Library of Congress Cataloging-in-Publication Data is available
ISBN 9781513262260

Editor: Michelle McCann
Designer: Vicki Knapton

WestWinds Press®
An imprint of

GRAPHIC ARTS
BOOKS®

GraphicArtsBooks.com

Proudly distributed by Ingram Publisher Services

Printed in the U.S.A.

2018 LSI

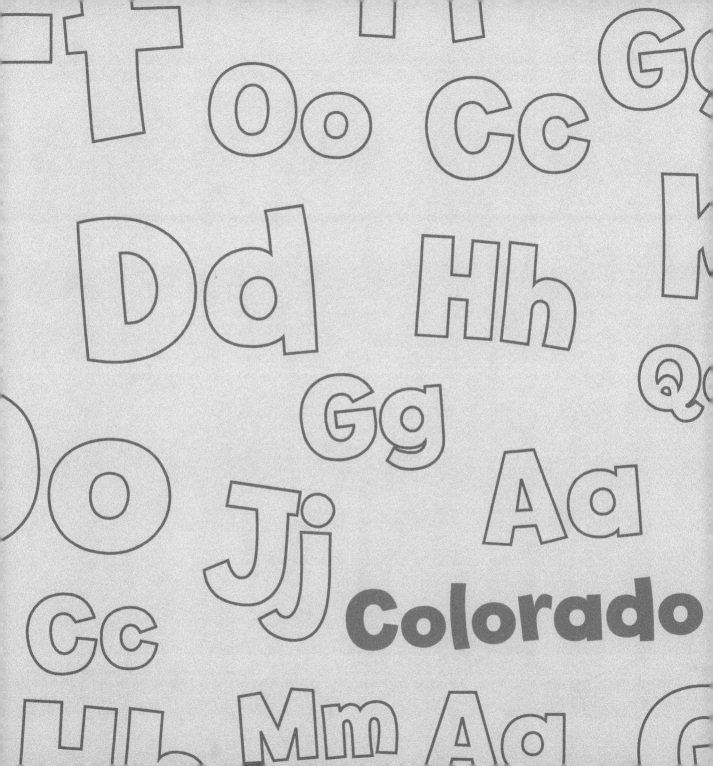

Printed in the USA
CPSIA information can be obtained
at www.ICGtesting.com
JSHW072020140824
68134JS00040B/3713